This bOOK Belongs to... HERD

This book is dedicated to the very special Michael and Nora.

 Thank You to
PAT. David.
bEn + Emily
and Ellis + JOBey

WHO'S AFRAID OF THE BIG BAD BOOK
by Lauren Child

British Library Cataloguing in Publication
Data. A catalogue record of this book is
available from the British Library.

ISBN : 978 0 340 80555 8

Copyright © Lauren Child 2002

The right of Lauren Child to be
identified as the author and illustrator
of this Work has been asserted by her in
accordance with the Copyright, Designs
and Patents Act 1988.

First edition published 2002
This paperback edition first published 2003
20 19 18 17 16 15 14 13

Published by Hodder Children's Books
a division of Hachette Children's Books
338 Euston Road London NW1 3BH

Originated by Dot Gradations Ltd, UK

Printed in Singapore

Who's Afraid of The Big Bad Book?

Lauren Child

Hodder
Children's
Books

A division of Hachette Children's Books

Herb loved storybooks.

Although he wasn't a very good reader, it didn't matter because he could tell a lot from the pictures. Herb liked the scary ones best with pictures of dinosaurs gobbling up other dinosaurs, or swooping vampires chasing people who had foolishly decided to go for a midnight stroll without any garlic.

Herb read his books everywhere. This was why many of the pages were stickily stuck together, soggy round the edges and usually had bits of banana, biscuit and the odd pea squashed between the pages.

On this particular night,
Herb's friend Ezzie was staying over.
Earlier, the two of them had been playing
a game, involving a great deal of

untidying things

and, by the evening,

Herb

had trouble even finding his bed.

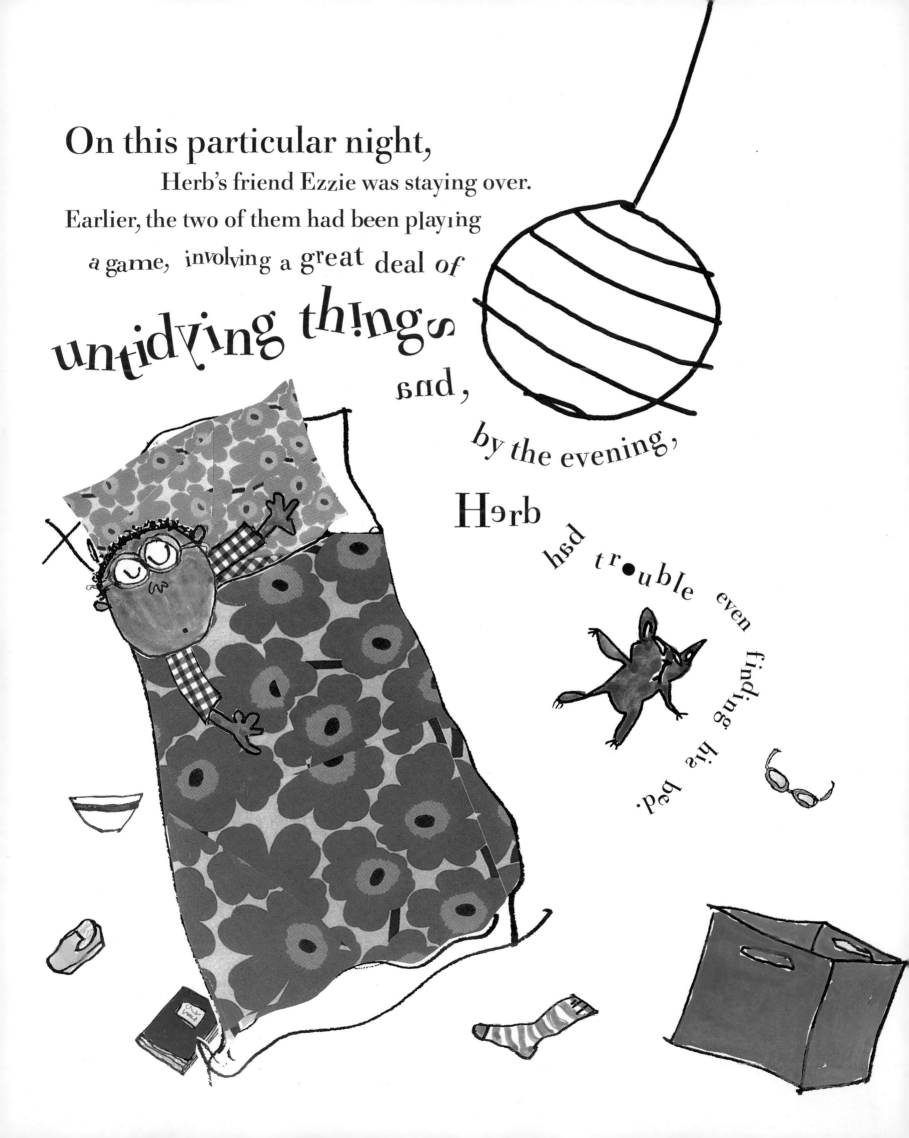

By the time he had, Ezzie was already slightly snoring. So Herb searched around for a book to amuse him until he dozed off but the only one he managed to find was

a book of **fairy tales.**

It hadn't been looked at in a very long time and was quite dusty. It was actually quite exciting but even so Herb's eyes soon became **heavy** and, before he could close the book, he fell asleep with his head on the page.

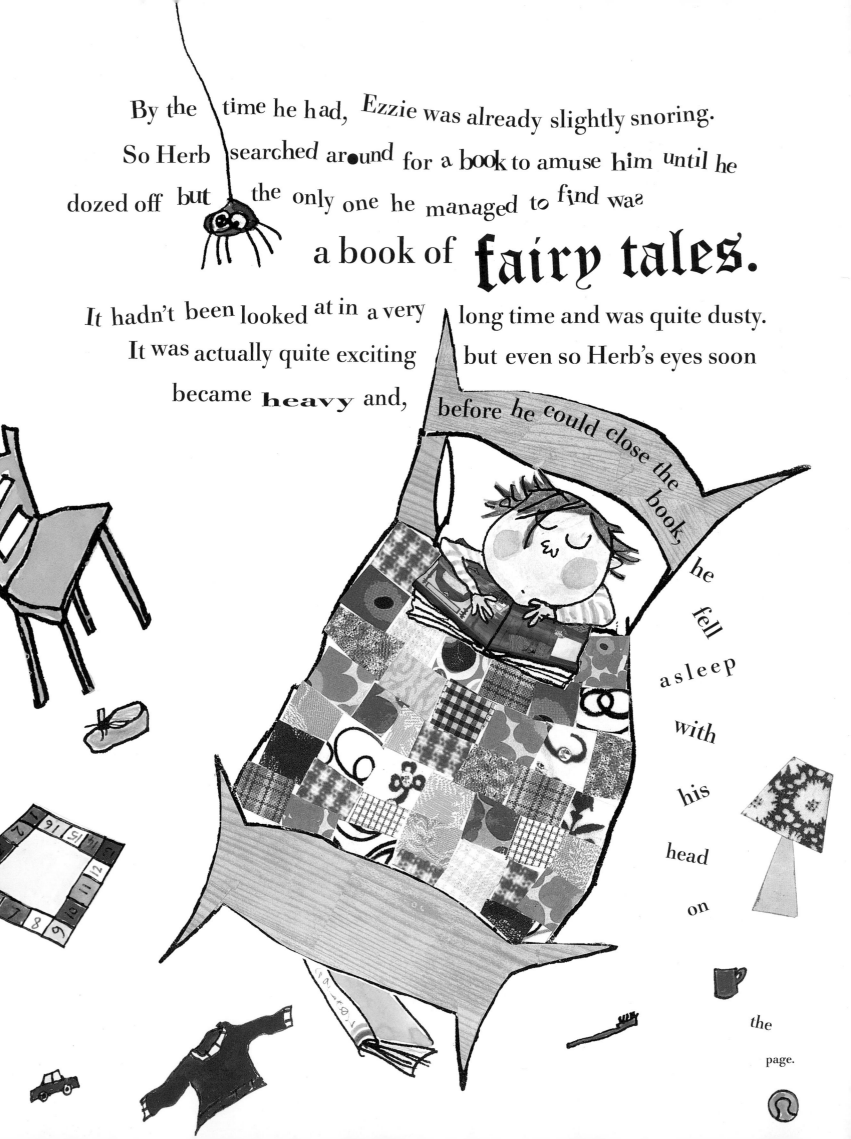

Herb woke with a start to hear a strange high-pitched shrieking noise. He looked over to see if Ezzie was awake but there was no sign of him at all. Furthermore, his bed had become sort of lumpy and huge, which was funny because Herb had always found his bed to be just right.

'WHAT ARE YOU DOING HERE? HOW DARE YOU BE ON THIS PAGE? I AM THE STAR AND I SAY YOU ARE NOT ALLOWED IN THIS STORY!' shrieked the shrieking thing.

'Wwwhere am I?' stammered Herb.

'ON MY PAGE!' screeched the girl.

'But who are you?' asked Herb, not sure that he wanted to know. 'I,' said the little girl, somehow managing to raise her voice even higher,

Herb scrabbled out of the bed as fast as he could, scooted down the stairs and went ... *slap, bang, wallop!* ... into three differently-sized bears.

'Whoops! I'm so sorry,' squeaked Herb terrified. 'I didn't mean to be here.'

'Oh, that's quite all right,' said the largest bear. 'It could happen to anyone.'

'And does all the time,' said the small bear, scowling at Goldilocks.

'**Ahem, hem!**'
coughed Goldilocks.
'IN CASE YOU PEA BRAINS
HAVE FORGOTTEN, THIS
STORY IS CALLED
"GOLDILOCKS AND
THE THREE BEARS"
NOT "THE LITTLE
SHOW-OFF IN
PYJAMAS HAS
BREAKFAST!"'

'How about some porridge?'
said the medium-sized bear.

'You might find it
too hot or too cold.

I'm afraid we're
out of just right.'

*Herb ran
for it!*

He ran past two children nibbling a house made of ginger biscuits. 'I wouldn't do that!' called Herb. **'Oh, get lost!'** shouted the children.

He ran past a man climbing up what looked like a long plait of hair. **'*Ouch!*'** cried the voice belonging to the hair.

Herb ran all the way

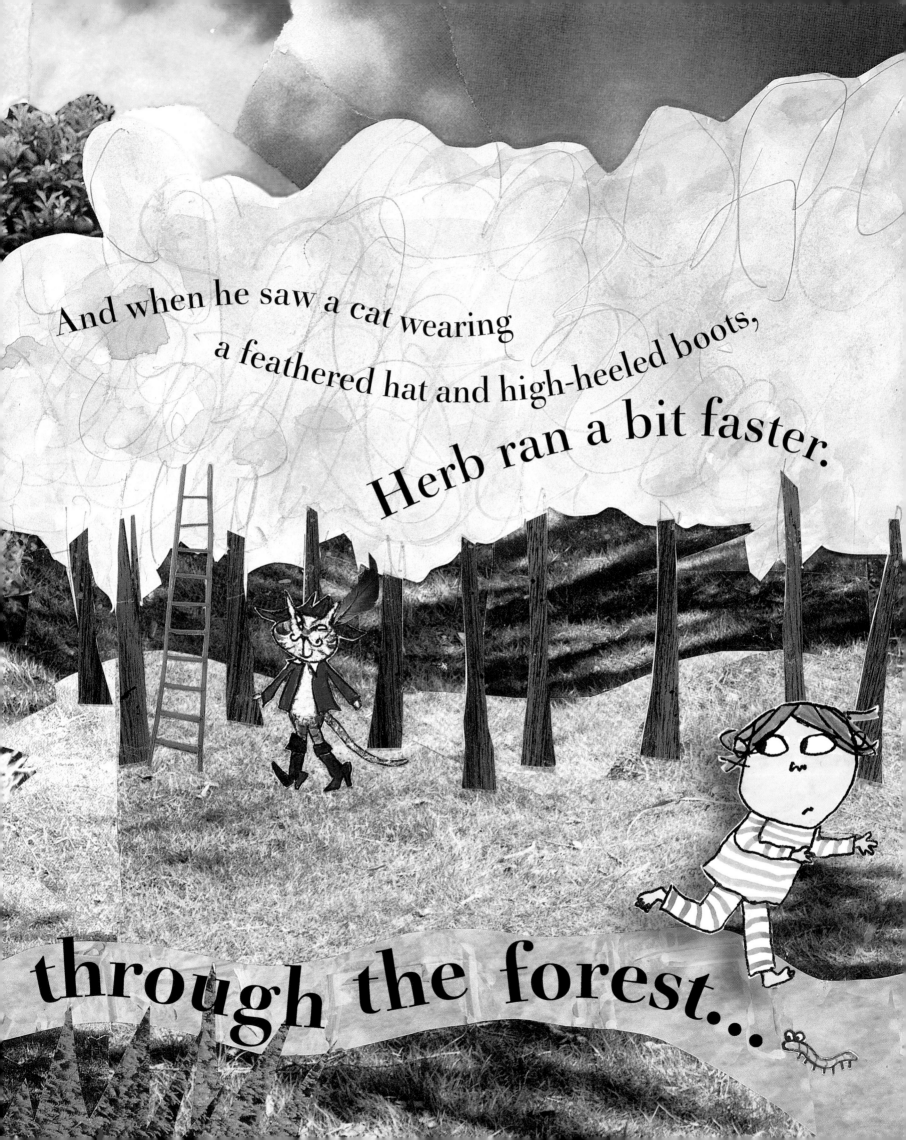

And when he saw a cat wearing a feathered hat and high-heeled boots, Herb ran a bit faster.

through the forest...

AT LONG LAST,
HE CAME TO AN
ENORMOUS DOOR.
IT WAS DIFFICULT TO
OPEN BECAUSE THE
ILLUSTRATOR HAD
DRAWN THE HANDLE
MUCH TOO HIGH UP
BUT, AFTER THREE
ATTEMPTS AT
JUMPING, HERB
MANAGED TO GRAB IT
AND SLOWLY CREAK
THE DOOR OPEN.

As Herb wondered desperately what to do next, he noticed his
pencil case lying on the floor; he'd been looking for it for months.
'It's all right, I can draw you a new throne,' he said.
'*Make sure it's got lots of twirly bits,*' blustered the king.
'*And I want it gold, of course,*' ordered the queen.
Herb didn't have a gold crayon; it would have to be green.
The queen did not look impressed.
Then, finding the eraser, Herb started to rub away at the queen's moustache.

'*Ow, ow, OW! That really hurts!*
Seize him!' she roared.

Herb made a dash for it.

There wasn't time to get to the door but, by snipping a hole in the
palace floor, Herb managed to wriggle through onto the next page.
He could hear the queen shouting, '*Look, he's at it again!*'

Herb found himself in an oddly arranged room.

'Who are you? You measly little rodent.'

Looking up, Herb saw Cinderella's wickedly mean stepmother and her ugly daughters.

'I'm Herb,' called Herb. 'What are you doing up there?'

'I wonder... are we pretending to be flies...?' scoffed the woman, 'or could it be that some some vile good-for-nothing child tore out our page and put it back upside down?'

'I wonder who would do that?' said Herb, slightly blushing.

'Probably some hideous little boy,'

snarled the stepmother, fixing Herb with her beady eyes.

'Now we can't get to the ball and Prince Charming can't fall madly, utterly in love with us. It's so unfair,' whined the pudgy sister.

'He wouldn't look twice at you,' snapped the skinny one.

'Oh do be quiet,' hissed the stepmother. 'I'm feeling queasy.'

Just then the telephone started to ring.

Sticking telephones in fairy tales had seemed funny at the time, but Herb could see that they could turn out to be rather a nuisance.

'Hello? Why hello your majesty… Yesss… as a matter of fact there is a little pyjamared boy here. He did what?… Oh he did, did he? Don't worry, I'll deal with the little weasel…' she said, giving Herb a shrivelling look. 'Oh, and by the way, if you see that nosy Goldilocks brat tell her to bring a ladder over.'

'So this is your doing!'
she screamed, leaping onto her chair.

'I'm going to make
you wish you'd never
opened a book!'

Herb speedily drew a
door on the wall, ran through it
and slammed it shut.

'Come back here
you little
horror!'

she screeched.

Herb was in a very dusty kitchen. His feet were sticking to the floor and there were what looked like giant biscuit crumbs stuck all over the place.

'Sorry about the dirt,' said a bedraggled-yet-pretty girl.

'Aren't you meant to be at the royal ball?' asked Herb.

'Yes, but I had to come home because the prince, achoo…, was late and my party dress dissolved into rags and I really looked, achoo…, a mess and then my carriage turned back into a pumpkin, which was sort of embarrassing. Would you like a cup of, achoo…, tea?'

She really was very nice and Herb
was beginning to feel extremely guilty,

because he had just remembered
where Prince Charming was:

Herb had cut him out to make
a birthday card for his mother.

'If only I could get out of
this book I could find
the prince for you,' he said.

'Ooh.... I know
who can help,'
said Cinderella,

picking up
her phone.

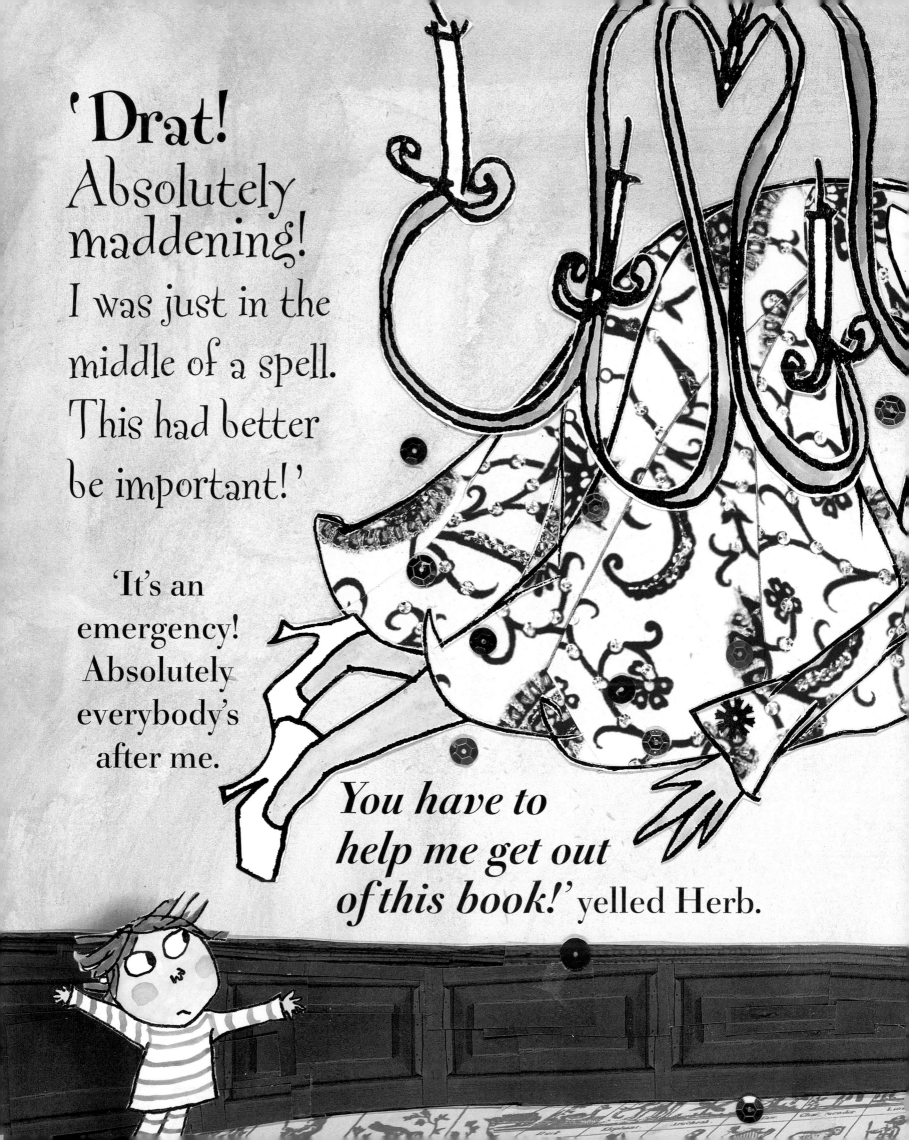

'Drat! Absolutely maddening! I was just in the middle of a spell. This had better be important!'

'It's an emergency! Absolutely everybody's after me.

You have to help me get out of this book!' yelled Herb.

'Well let me see...

A. Are you my fairy godchild?

No, you are not. I don't do boys; only girls worst luck.

B. What do you expect when you go about scribbling and snippering and generally causing mayhem?

This is no way to treat a book you know!

And C...

jumping into other people's stories, really is very rude.'

'But I can't find my way out,' pleaded Herb, near his wits' end.

'All right, all right, keep your pyjamas on. I suppose I'll have to come to the rescue as always. Now where did I put my wand?'

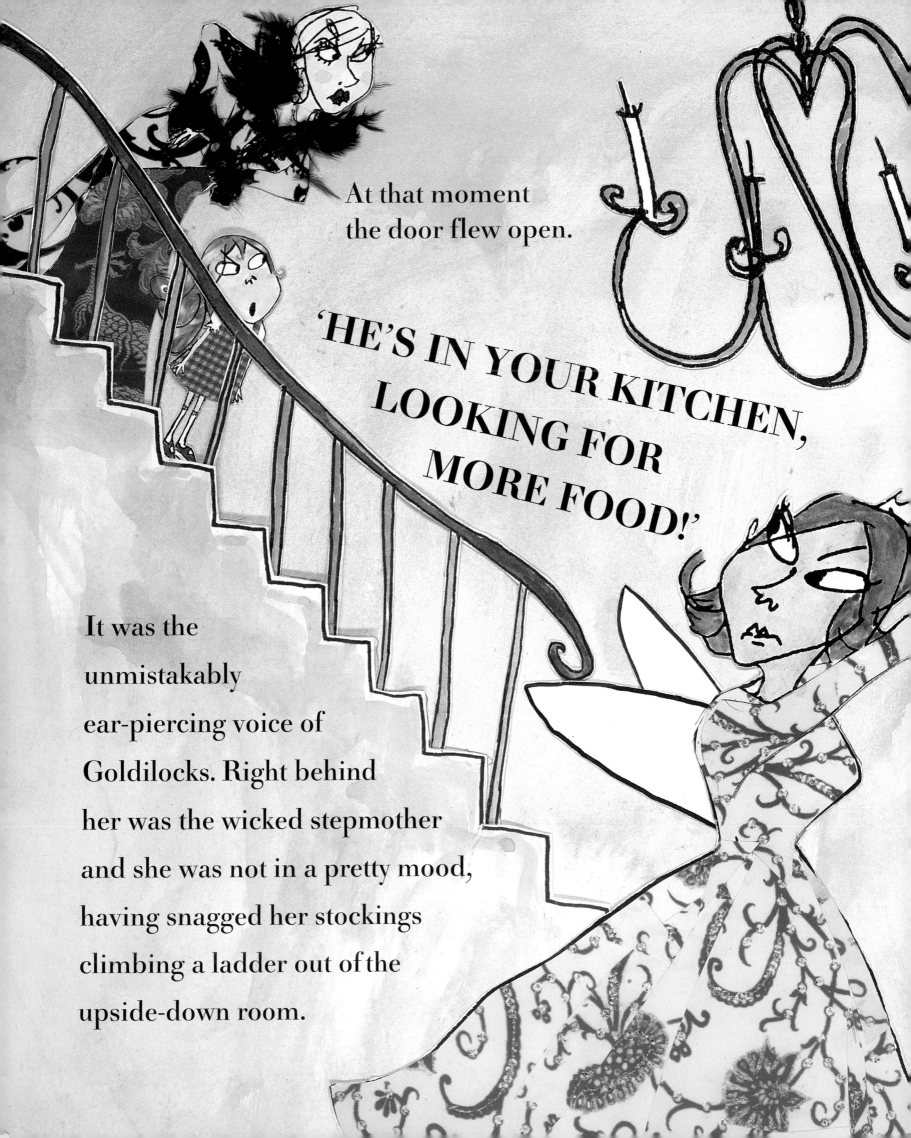

At that moment
the door flew open.

'HE'S IN YOUR KITCHEN,
LOOKING FOR
MORE FOOD!'

It was the
unmistakably
ear-piercing voice of
Goldilocks. Right behind
her was the wicked stepmother
and she was not in a pretty mood,
having snagged her stockings
climbing a ladder out of the
upside-down room.

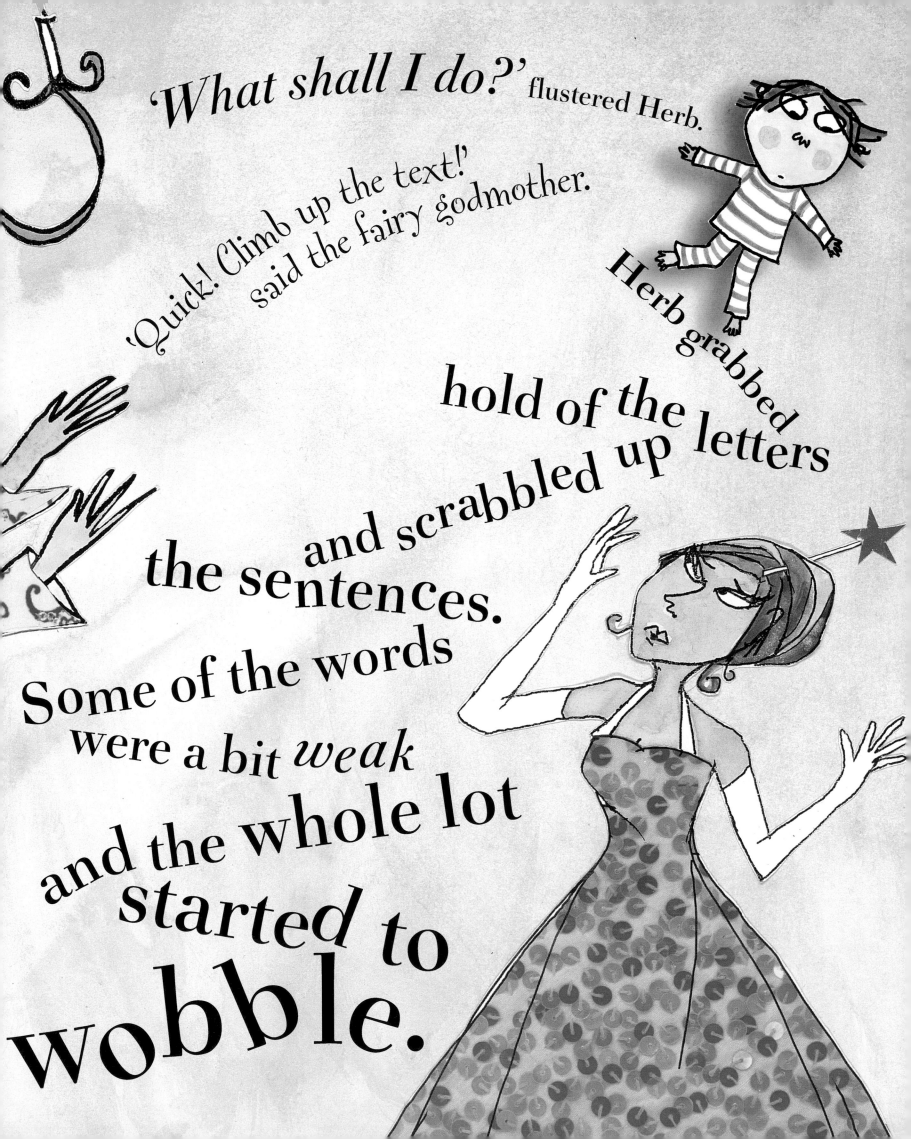

'What shall **I** do?' flustered Herb.

'Quick! Climb up the text!' said the fairy godmother.

Herb grabbed

hold of the letters

and scrabbled up

the sentences.

Some of the words were a bit *weak*

and the whole lot started to

wobble.

... screamed Goldilocks so loudly that the whole book shook and slipped off the bed, sending Herb falling headlong through the air onto ...

. . . his own bedroom floor.

'Wh-what's happening?' squeaked a startled Ezzie, sitting bolt upright in bed. As you can imagine it all took some explaining.

Ezzie and Herb spent the rest of the night putting the storybook back to rights: rubbing out moustaches cleaning out crumbs and blowing away dust. The bewildered Prince Charming was prised off the birthday card and sticky-taped back into the ballroom. His dancing would never quite be the same again due to severe leg creasing.

It was tempting to leave the wicked stepmother's room upside-down, but Herb resisted. However, he just couldn't help drawing a padlock on the three bears' front door. And Ezzie just couldn't help sticking a wig on Goldilocks. Well, serves her right for being such a meany.

...and they all lived happily ever after

The End

So, the next time Herb opened the book, he saw
a little girl standing outside the three bears' cottage
desperately trying to open the door —

a very cross little girl with mousey brown hair.